# A Penny and
# Two Fried Eggs
## & Other Stories

••

# A Penny and Two Fried Eggs

## & Other Stories

◆ ◆

Geraldine Gross Harder

Illustrated by Holly Hannon

HERALD PRESS
Scottdale, Pennsylvania
Waterloo, Ontario

**Library of Congress Cataloging-in-Publication Data**
Harder, Geraldine Gross.
  A penny and two fried eggs and other stories   /
Geraldine Gross Harder.
      p.    cm.
  Summary: Profiles the lives and contributions of four
Mennonite leaders, Christopher Dock, Christian
Krehbiel, David Rittenhouse, and Henry Smith.
    ISBN 0-8361-3564-4 (alk. paper)
    1. Mennonites—United States—Biography—Juvenile
literature. I. Title.
BX8141.H37   1991
289.7'092'2—dc20
[B]                                             91-16999
                                                    CIP
                                                     AC

The paper used in this publication is recycled and
meets the minimum requirements of American National
Standard for Information Sciences—Permanence of
Paper for Printed Library Materials. ANSI Z39.48-1984.

Scripture quotations are from the *Good News Bible*, Old
Testament copyright © 1976, by the American Bible
Society.

# To

Olive Moyer Gross, my mother and first teacher, who herself was an elementary school teacher and encouraged me to be a teacher.

Emily B. Long, my first grade teacher, who inspired me to be a teacher.

Mary Royer, one of my Goshen College professors, who helped me on my way to teach and write.

Sadie Ruth, a Sunday school teacher during my teens who left a lasting positive impression upon my life.

Our son Bob and his wife, Lorna, and our son Jim and his wife, Karen, all of whom are college teachers, and all teachers, who affect eternity. No one can ever tell where their influence stops.

All children everywhere who dream of being teachers someday.

# Contents

# PART ONE

# A Penny and
# Two Fried Eggs

# Contents

# 1

# The Praying Schoolmaster

Come, let's pretend we can see through the window of a little schoolhouse in Skippack, Pennsylvania. The window is made of paper that is greased and oiled.

School is out. I think I can see the old schoolmaster, Christopher Dock. Can you? He is tidying up the room and getting the lessons ready for tomorrow.

It is autumn, 1771, more than 200 years ago, and the leaves are falling. They are golden and pretty beyond the clearing where the schoolhouse stands. Not far away the Skippack Creek skips merrily over the smooth pebbles and shows rainbow colors.

The sun is setting low in the sky. Schoolteacher Dock stands for a moment at the door with a broom in his hand. We can see him better now.

He notices the paint-box tints in the sky and likes the evening picture God has made. Christopher Dock loves beautiful colors and likes to draw pictures himself.

He is thinking of the children who have gone home. "Keep their lives beautiful like your sky," he prays to God.

Christopher Dock puts the broom in the corner and kneels at his desk. He opens his roll book to the names of his pupils. Then he folds his hands and looks up toward heaven as he prays for each one.

"Thank you for Henry, who did such good work with his numbers today.

"Bless Eli. He blew in his inkwell and soiled Emily's clothing. Help him to take his schoolwork more seriously so he will not have time for pranks.

"Bless Sarah and Margaret. They were good helpers and kept their minds on what they were doing.

"Bless John. He is so lazy, and bless Elizabeth who finds it hard to learn.

"Please forgive me if I did not notice someone who was lonely or sad or afraid. Help me to be wiser tomorrow as I teach these children, who are also your children.

"Watch over each child on the way home, and help them all to have a pleasant evening with their families. May they not forget to pray."

Across the years we listen at the windows or at the door of the little log schoolhouse in the clearing. Every evening after school we hear Schoolteacher Dock's voice praying for his pupils. How much he loved them!

Christopher Dock was a very old man now. On one of those autumn evenings, he was talking with God about his pupils as usual. Just then he slumped to the floor in his schoolroom and stopped breathing.

It fit his way of life for him to die at the end of day on his knees, at prayer in the schoolroom where he gave himself in teaching. Like Enoch in the Bible, he had walked with God every day.

How much his pupils missed him! They loved him because they felt his love for them. His eyes and voice were kind. Love shone out of their schoolteacher and all around him.

His pupils could not forget him, and the people in the community never forgot him either. We, too, cannot forget him after we have heard the story of Christopher Dock.

# 2

# Christoph in Germany

We do not know exactly where Christopher Dock came from or who his parents were. No one knows if he had brothers or sisters. We do know, though, that he grew up somewhere in Germany near the Rhine River.

Let's try to imagine what Christopher Dock was like as a boy.

It is early evening in the German village where Christoph lives. No one has had supper because the farmers have not yet come home from the fields.

Christoph likes the end of day. The lumbering wagons will soon clatter down the cobblestone street with their loads of newly cut hay. How clean and sweet it will smell! At last Christoph hears the faint sound of wagon wheels.

"*Mutter!* The wagons are coming! I hear them!"

Mother smiles away her tiredness. She has had a busy day with the laundry. It is hard work to rub and scrub the clothes clean.

Mother likes the end of day, too, when the whole family is together for *Abendbrot* (supper).

The sinking sun smiles down on the hay wagons coming home.

Soon it is suppertime. Christoph's father asks God to bless the food. Then all hold hands and say heartily, "*Guten Appetit!*"

How good the *Wurst* (sausage) and the fresh lettuce taste, the new potatoes with their jackets on, and the sweet milk!

Christoph does not smack his lips. He eats quietly and cleans out his bowl carefully. He wipes his mouth and hands on his napkin.

Father says "Thank you" for the good meal to Mother and to God.

Then Christoph knows he is excused. He bows when he leaves the room.

# 3

# The Trip
# to America

Sometimes while Christoph herded geese, he did a lot of thinking.

"I want to be a kind schoolteacher some day," he told the geese.

His friends honked loudly as if to say, "Yes, we know you will be kind. We know because you are kind to us and care about us."

Later, Christoph did become a teacher for four years in Germany, but it was hard for him to teach there. The state had taken over the schools from the church.

Teachers were strict and often punished their pupils cruelly. Christoph was not this kind of teacher. He knew that children should be taught in a kind and loving way.

Christoph also knew that he could not fight in a war. He wished to live in a land where he could practice peace and live out his faith in God.

So when Christoph Dock was in his twenties, he got on a big ship that sailed to America. There he could live and work in a way that would please God.

The trip to America was difficult. It took many weeks to cross the ocean, and there was not enough food. It was chilly on the ship, and there were storms. The ship rocked this way and that, and salt water dashed in over the sides. People got sick, and many of them died.

Christoph was thankful when at last they docked in Philadelphia. The year was 1718. In America he soon found that people who spoke English called him Christopher.

The young schoolteacher could hardly wait to start teaching again. As soon as he could, he went to a village along the Skippack Creek about thirty miles north of Philadelphia.

Christoph liked the name of the village, Skippack, which means "ship's creek." A stream in Holland and two villages in Germany carry that same name.

Christoph's heart beat faster when he

saw the little log schoolhouse in the clearing. The evening sun was shining against the oiled and greased windows, and they looked like pots of gold.

Christoph had decided that he wanted to teach children as long as he lived, and here was his first schoolhouse in America! He wondered who his first pupils would be.

Christoph breathed deeply of the fresh air of Penn's Woods. It looked a lot like Germany, where he lived before. The dark woods and the rolling hills were the same, but the laws were different.

Now Christoph could teach pupils the truths God gave him. That is why he sighed contentedly. He was so glad that God had given him this wonderful home where he could teach children in a kind and loving way!

**4**

# First Day
of School

Samuel was one of Christopher Dock's pupils. One fall, on the first day of school, Samuel walked through the woods to the little schoolhouse in the clearing. His shoes kicked up some of the early leaves that had already fallen.

Samuel popped a late plump blackberry into his mouth. The juice was good and sweet. A rabbit scampered off into the underbrush.

A blue jay scolded from the top of a tree. "Now don't be late! Now don't be late!"

"You know I won't! You know I won't!" Samuel singsonged back to the jay. "It's my first day, and I don't want to be late."

Samuel wondered how school would go

and if he would like the new teacher. People said the man was kind and that he loved children.

"I hope Christopher Dock will like me," Samuel said to any animals listening to him there in the woods.

Samuel ran the rest of the way. When he came to the edge of the clearing, he saw the teacher standing in the door of the little log schoolhouse.

The teacher had long hair to his shoulders, a V-shaped collar, and breeches to his knees. There were buckles on his shoes, too.

Samuel noticed all these things, but he kept looking at Christopher Dock's face. It was so kind!

Samuel's heart thumped when Christopher Dock called him. The teacher's voice was the kindest voice Samuel had ever heard.

"Good morning to you," said Christopher Dock cheerily. "Let's see. Is your name Samuel?"

"Yes, sir." Samuel bowed low.

Christopher Dock shook his hand and then all of the other children shook his hand, too.

Samuel's teacher handed him a note. "This says, 'Industrious: one penny,'" he told Samuel. "You are now a pupil in our school.

"You shall have a penny if you are industrious, which means that you are to keep busy at your work and do it well. I shall expect you to be obedient, too. You look like you will try very hard."

Samuel gave his teacher a broad smile and looked around the schoolroom. It was such a friendly place. He saw beautiful drawings on the wall and wondered who had made them.

"Sometimes children forget what the note says and become lazy, Samuel," Christopher Dock went on. "Then I must take the note away."

"I will try not to forget," promised Samuel. He was not a bit afraid of this teacher. Samuel knew he could trust him, and he wanted so much to please him! Samuel wanted to keep his note forever.

Then Christopher Dock told Samuel some rules to remember at school:

"Always obey your teacher, and do not make him remind you of the same thing many times.

"Act lovingly and peacefully toward your schoolmates. Do not quarrel with them, hit them, dirty their clothes with your shoes or ink, nor give them nicknames. Act toward them as you would like them to act toward you.

"Keep your books clean inside and out. Do not scribble or draw in them. Do not lose or tear them."

Samuel thought about the rules. He wanted to remember them all.

Samuel noticed that some poor children attended school, too, and that Christopher Dock was just as kind to them. Samuel's father would pay Christopher Dock five shillings each week. Father had said that not all of the parents could afford to do this.

But the school was open to every child because the master from Skippack had said, "That is all right. All children should be able to learn to read and write."

Samuel now knew that what people said about Christopher Dock was true. He was kind, and he did love children.

Samuel sighed happily. He was going to like school very, very much.

# 5

# Rewards!

Soon Samuel could say his A-B-Cs and point out any letter.

"What is this letter?" asked Christopher Dock as he pointed to the wall with a stick.

"An *M*," Samuel answered.

"And this one?"

"A *P*."

"You may go into the A-B-C class now," said Christopher Dock, "and I will write a note for your parents." The schoolteacher from Skippack gave Samuel a big smile.

The bigger children in the school had joy on their faces, too. They remembered how it felt when they were promoted into the A-B-C class and Christopher Dock was pleased with them. Then they could take a note home to their parents. Happiness was everywhere in the room.

At noon while they were eating their lunch, Wesley told Samuel, "Good for you. Next you will learn to read. Then the teacher will give you a certificate. Maybe it will have a bird on it. Or it may even be one of the mottoes on the wall."

Samuel looked at the lovely pictures on the wall that Christopher Dock had drawn. The writing was so neat. He wished he could read the words.

Wesley told him that one of the mottoes said, "A friend loveth at all times."

Samuel liked that motto. It had two beautiful birds on it. The birds were flying side by side, like good friends. One did not try to go faster than the other. There were bright colors on the picture, especially greens and reds.

Samuel often looked at the pictures during the day.

That evening Samuel carried his precious note home to his parents. He wondered what it said. He did not want to lose it.

Mother read the note first. "Samuel knows his A-B-Cs," she read. "His father owes him a penny now, and his mother

The teacher gave Samuel a certificate for learning his
A-B-Cs.

must fry him two eggs."

Mother smiled as broadly as she could and gave Samuel a kiss. "That's fine," she said. "Can you say your A-B-Cs for me?"

Samuel did, and he said them perfectly. Father came into the kitchen just as Samuel finished with the Z. Mother handed Father the note to read. Then Father wanted to hear Samuel say the A-B-Cs all over again.

For supper that night Samuel had two delicious fried eggs, and there was a penny at his plate. Father was proud of his six-year-old son.

What nice rewards! The eggs tasted especially good, and now he had a penny of his very own! It was the first penny that Samuel ever owned.

# 6

# Story Time
# at School

Samuel had to walk a long way to school. Many other children did, too, so at noon it felt good to rest a little after lunch.

During the rest period, some of the older boys and girls took turns reading stories from the Old Testament. Samuel liked the stories about Joseph and David. But the best story for him was the one about Samuel, because they both had the same name.

Samuel, the boy in the Bible, helped Eli in the temple and heard God calling his name in the middle of the night. God called him three times! He had something important to tell him, and Samuel listened with care.

The children in Christopher Dock's school

spoke German, and they learned to read German, too. Their grammar book had some English words alongside the German, and the pupils were starting to pick up a little English.

They did not have many books, but most of all, the parents wanted them to be able to read the Bible well.

Christopher Dock was the first teacher in America to use a blackboard. He blackened a piece of board and used chalk on it. He used the blackboard to help his pupils learn their numbers.

Christopher Dock's school was always in good order. It was clean and neat. Children kept their belongings in the proper place.

The children said their prayers slowly and carefully and thought of what they were saying.

No one tried to talk the loudest. When the teacher asked questions, they raised their hands. If he called on a pupil, that one would stand to reply.

If someone used bad words, Christopher Dock asked, "Did you think up the words yourself or did you hear them from someone else?"

"I heard them from someone else."

"Try not to use the words again," Christopher Dock said kindly.

Christopher Dock taught his pupils to read and he taught them their numbers. But he also taught them many other things. That is why Christopher Dock's school was such a happy place. It was full of loving and learning.

# 7

# Blackberry Cake

Margaret and Catherine were Christopher Dock's two little daughters. They liked to play under the big oak trees on Father's farm near Skippack. The wide curling roots that grew on top of the ground made a little house where the girls could play.

"What could we use for dishes?" asked Catherine one day. "Mother would not want us to use hers."

"These acorn cups would make perfect dishes," suggested Margaret as she picked some up from under the oak trees. "There are ripe berries now. Let's pick some and have a party with our dolls."

After the girls set the table with acorn

Margaret and Catherine were having a party with
their rag dolls, Priscilla and Matilda.

dishes, they walked partway into the woods. They found some delicious blackberries! There were huckleberries and wild grapes, too.

"We will have a wonderful party!" exclaimed Catherine.

"I have an idea," suggested Margaret. "After we have our party, let's pick some berries for Mother. You know how she said we must all help Father. He had to stop teaching because he could not earn enough money now that we are in the family."

"Couldn't the people pay?"

"Oh, sometimes they did, but Father could not count on it. He decided to farm for a while, but I am sure he will teach again."

After the girls had enough berries for their party, they ran to their home in the clearing to find their rag dolls. Soon four little girls were having a party—Margaret and Catherine, and Priscilla and Matilda.

The berries tasted even better in the acorn cups!

After the party the girls picked berries for a long time. It was quiet and pretty in the woods. The berries for Mother plopped into their pails.

When they came home, Mother was so

glad for the berries! She gave them each a hug.

"I will make a blackberry cake," she said. "Father will be pleased."

While the girls were picking blackberries, Father was plowing.

Christopher Dock had bought a farm from the Penn brothers. William Penn, one of the brothers, was the founder of the Commonwealth of Pennsylvania. Father's farm had 100 acres of land. He paid fifteen English pounds and ten shillings for it.

Several white oak trees and three posts were boundary markers for his farm. There were nice woods on the farm, and nuts grew there as well as berries and fruit.

At last the girls saw Father coming home. "Surprise, Father!" the girls shouted when Father came into the yard. "We're going to have a surprise for supper!"

Father tried to guess. "Corn pone?"

"No." The girls' eyes sparkled.

"Blackberries and milk?"

"No, but you are getting closer."

Father could not guess, and the girls made Father wait until dessert time. Then Mother set a fragrant blackberry cake on the table in front of Father.

"Oh!" exclaimed Father. "So this is the surprise! It smells delicious!"

"We picked the berries," Catherine told Father. "Margaret and I did."

Everyone enjoyed the tasty cake that Mother had made.

"I'm glad that God thought about putting blackberry bushes in the woods," said Margaret.

"And I'm glad that Mother knows how to make blackberry cake," added Catherine.

"I think God taught Mother how to do that," Father said with a big grin as he finished eating his cake.

Mother's eyes twinkled as she looked across the table at Father. She agreed with him.

# 8

# Father, a Good Teacher

When Sunday came, Father said, "Don't forget your Bibles and hymnbooks, and listen carefully to the sermon!"

"We will remember," promised Margaret. "I will take my slate along and write down the things the minister says."

"Good," said Father. "After church I will read what you wrote."

Catherine was younger than Margaret and could not write well. But her father said that soon she could have a slate framed in wood.

Margaret had some slips of paper in her Bible. Father liked her to find the verse the minister was reading and to mark the place in her Bible.

Catherine watched where Margaret put her slips, and she put some slips in her Bible at the same place.

The girls liked it when their father led the singing at their church. They knew he had even written some of the hymns they sang.

Margaret and Catherine never talked in church. Father would not be pleased.

Sometimes the girls got sleepy. It helped if they stood up for a while. Father said they could do this.

When the service was over, they visited with friends. Then they went home, ate lunch, and rested for a while.

Each morning the girls got up as soon as Mother called. They turned back the covers on their bed and put on their clothes quickly and neatly.

While they were getting dressed, they thought about God. Father had said that was a good idea. There was something about Father that made you want to do the things he suggested.

The night before, Mother had filled the white pitcher on top of the nightstand with clean water. It made a gurgling sound when the girls poured it into the big bowl. They tried not to splash water when they washed their faces.

Margaret thanked God for a pretty day, and Catherine thanked him for the nice acorns they could use for play dishes.

When they first awoke, the girls said "Good morning" to each other. Later they said "Good morning" to Mother and Father when they came for breakfast.

There were smiles on their faces and love in their voices. Father said greetings should be this way. It would help everyone to have a nice day.

Mother helped the girls to braid their hair.

During breakfast Father said, "I'm glad my girls remember to let others finish talking before they say something. I was at the Yoder farm the other day, and one of the boys kept talking while his father and I were visiting."

"Perhaps his father does not teach him as well as you teach us," said Margaret.

"Father *is* a good teacher," praised Mother. "I hope he can teach school again soon. The Skippack children need his help."

Father smiled.

Margaret and Catherine did not always remember to follow Father's good rules, but most of the time they pleased their parents well.

# 9

# Cheery Evenings

Margaret and Catherine liked the cheery evenings at home. The warm flames in the fireplace felt good, and there were songs to sing and tales to hear. Father was good at telling stories.

"Tell the one about Moses, when he was a baby," Catherine sometimes begged as she climbed up on Father's lap.

Then Father would begin: "Many years ago there was a little girl about as big as you whose name was Miriam. She had a little brother named Aaron and a tiny baby brother."

While Father told the story, Margaret sat at his knee. Mother did some sewing. They all liked to hear Father's kind voice telling a story. They could see the word pictures he drew for them.

After the story and some hymns and a prayer, Catherine and Margaret snuggled under their covers. Tomorrow they would help Mother make candles, but there would be time to play in the friendly woods, too.

Penn's Woods was a beautiful place all year round. In deep winter, snow covered the evergreen branches and stuck to the tall, slim, leafless trees. Dainty animal tracks made designs on top of the snow blanket.

In spring, flowers waited to be made into bouquets for the mothers who lived near Skippack.

One summer evening Catherine and Margaret were making plans for the next day. Before playing they would look in the fields on Father's farm for the milkweed pods with their silky down. Mother used it to make wicks for the candles.

The girls liked to watch Mother slip the milkweed over a candle rod and dip it into the melted tallow. The tallow clung to the wick. Mother kept on dipping until the candle she was making was thick enough.

"I hope Mother will let us make a tiny candle to put on our playhouse table under the oak tree," Margaret said to Catherine.

"I hope so, too," answered Catherine just as she fell asleep.

# 10

# A Teacher Again

Christopher Dock did teach again. This time he taught at two schools—for three days at Skippack and for three more days at Salford. That made a full week.

The teacher from Skippack liked to ride his horse to school on the days he taught at Salford. God seemed near as he and his horse trotted along.

Christopher Dock hummed hymns to himself and noticed the new flowers growing in the spring. He could almost see the leaves on the trees growing a little bigger each day.

In his pocket he carried letters from the children at Skippack addressed to the pupils at Salford. The children could hardly wait for the postman to come.

They liked to read their letters, but they also loved their schoolteacher. They wished school could be every day.

The children at Skippack were glad for the letters their postman-teacher brought from Salford. The first day of school in the new week was always a special day.

Sometimes Christopher Dock also did other work besides teaching. He cleaned the graveyard of the Skippack Mennonite congregation. It took a lot of work to mow the grass and trim things neatly and carry away the clippings.

Christopher Dock wrote wills for people. People liked his handwriting. It was neat and easily read, and he could state things well on paper.

For treasured records, he wrote in a German style called Fraktur. On the edges of the paper he would draw pictures of birds and flowers for decoration.

Sometimes he served as a lawyer when a hearing came up. Everyone respected Christopher Dock.

One day he received a visit from Dielman Kolb, preacher of the Salford Mennonite Church. Kolb had an important letter from a printer in Germantown, near Philadelphia. This printer, Christopher Sauer, wanted a record of how Christopher Dock managed his school.

The letter had come to Kolb. "We would like you to write down Dock's good rules for teaching children," the letter said. "Other people should know about his rules and follow them. Our children need to learn their letters and to obey God."

Preacher Kolb came to ask his friend Christopher Dock to write about these things. The schoolteacher thought carefully about how to reply to the message in this letter.

He told Kolb he did not want to do anything for his own praise. But if his rules could be helpful, he would be willing to write them for others to read.

Christopher Dock also said he wanted Kolb and the printer to give him any tips that would help him to bring glory to God in his teaching.

That very day, August 8, 1750, he started to write about his way of teaching. Christopher Dock told how he showed love to his pupils and did not beat them, as other teachers did.

He explained how he kept order in the classroom and interested the children so they wanted to learn. Then he let them use what they learned, as in writing letters to each other and reading the letters they received.

And so, more than two hundred years ago, Christopher Dock prepared a small book about how to teach children. He called it *School Management.*

Schoolmaster Dock still had a worry when he turned his booklet over to Christopher Sauer. He feared that people would think he was trying to get glory for himself. And so he asked that his book not be printed until he died.

When Sauer saw how good the booklet was, he used parts of it in a magazine without naming the author.

Christopher Dock also put together "A Hundred Necessary Rules of Conduct for Children." He let Sauer print them.

Soon after that, he gave Sauer a second set of a hundred rules that told children how to act toward God, their neighbors, and themselves. Those were printed, too.

As Schoolmaster Dock kept writing, he saw how much people were helped by reading his letters and rules. His friends were begging to see more of his writings.

So then, twenty years after he wrote *School Management,* he let Sauer's son print the whole booklet. All the copies sold out quickly, and a second printing was done that same year, 1770, just one year before the beloved schoolmaster died.

*School Management* became famous as the first book on education in America. Many teachers read it and became better teachers.

In these stories you have read some of Christopher Dock's rules on how to behave at school, at home, and at church. Margaret and Catherine tried to live what their father taught.

Here are some more of his good rules:

1. Do not run about wildly on the street and shout, but walk quietly.

2. Do not walk along looking at the sky, do not run against people, and do not tread where the mud is thickest or in puddles.

3. Lay your books and other belongings in their proper places, and do not let them lie carelessly about.

4. Do not frown or have a sour look.

5. Do not be sulky when you are asked a question, but let others finish talking and do not interrupt them.

6. Do not answer by shaking or nodding your head, but answer with clear, kind words.

7. When you have made a promise, try to keep it.

Sauer printed these rules from Christopher Dock, and also *The Golden ABC of a Pious Child. Pious* means worshiping and obeying God.

For this book, Christopher Dock found Bible verses starting with the ABCs. In his German Bible, he could find a verse for every letter except *V, X,* and *Y.*

Christopher Dock was a good teacher because he was kind and loving like Jesus. Everyone loved Christopher Dock, and I think that now you know why because you know his story, too.

● ● ●

Your teachers and parents may wish to check a library for a book by Gerald C. Studer, *Christopher Dock: Colonial Schoolmaster: The Biography and Writings of Christopher Dock* (Herald Press, 1967). *The Mennonite Encyclopedia,* volume 2 (Herald Press, 1956), also tells about Christopher Dock.

# PART TWO

# The Song
# of the Hoofs

# Contents

# 1

# The Song of the Hoofs

*Trot-trot, trot-trot,* sang a black pony's hoofs as he frisked away down the road. *Trot-trot, trot-trot.* Christian Krehbiel watched the dust from the pony's heels as it made clouds in the air and settled to the road again.

Behind him a deep voice singsonged:

I wish young Chris could ride with me,
But he's not big enough, I see!

"Is that the pony's song?" asked Christian's Uncle Jacob, his eyes twinkling. "It won't be long, Chris, until you'll be riding that pony. But first you have a lot to learn."

"I know," mumbled Christian as he pushed his toes farther into the dirt and his hands deeper into the pockets of his leather pants. "I wish it wouldn't take me so long to grow up. I hope Schwartz (Blackie) can wait for me to ride her."

"Oh, she'll wait all right," laughed Uncle Jacob. "She had to wait a long time for the other boys to ride her. But they got along just fine. And you'll learn to ride her soon. Come, let's go to the stable. I'll teach you some things about the care of a pony."

Christian ran along beside his uncle. His eyes were bright now. *Surely, if Uncle is going to give me lessons in the stable, it might not be so long until I can ride Schwartz,* he thought happily.

Christian's days were busy now. There were chores to do and school lessons to learn. But there was time for play in the village streets of Weierhof in Germany, where Christian lived. Sometimes he would follow the river and watch the water pushing the mill wheel that made the power to grind the grain into flour.

Christian loved to run to the top of the hill and feel the great oak tree wrapping its branches around him, keeping him safe. Best of all, there was time for Christian to learn all about ponies.

Christian learned what Schwartz needed to eat to grow strong. He learned how to saddle Schwartz and how to curry her. He learned to say the words that made her go left and right and straight ahead.

"And remember, Chris," Uncle Jacob would say, "you must always have a sugar lump or two in your pocket for Schwartz. Then Schwartz will know you are pleased with her. And treat yourself to a sugar lump, too, my boy," Uncle Jacob added, laughing.

One day the calendar said that Christian was nine years old. Uncle Jacob's voice boomed from the stable: "Hop up on the saddle, my boy! You're off for a ride today!"

Christian came running like a streak of lightning. It was his important day. He had wished for this more than anything else in his whole life!

But Christian remembered just in time not to act excited when he came near Schwartz. He said some friendly words to Schwartz and stroked her gently.

Almost before he knew what was happening, he and Schwartz were trotting down the road, kicking up the dust behind them! The song of Schwartz's hoofs sounded different now:

Up and down went Christian and Schwartz in perfect
rhythm.

Young Chris is big enough today
To ride me very far away!

*Trot-trot, trot-trot. Trot-trot, trot-trot.* Up and down went Christian and Schwartz in perfect rhythm. Up and down. Up and down.

Christian's eyes were shining like stars when he brought Schwartz back to the stable.

"Well, how did it go?" asked Uncle Jacob in his deep voice.

"Fine," answered Christian. "Just fine."

Before long Christian was riding his uncle's horses, too. One day when they were out riding, the horse's hoofs got stuck in the mud. Christian had to let go of the reins when the horse stretched his neck and reared up to leap out.

The horse got out, but Christian slid off and was stuck in the mud up to his waist. Luckily, one of Christian's friends found the runaway horse. He looked for Christian and helped to pull him out of the mud.

Now Uncle Jacob made up another song:

Young Chris went riding far one day.
A-riding far went he.
But soon there was no horse in sight,
Just mud for Chris to see.

After Christian changed his clothes, he did not mind Uncle Jacob's song. He laughed about it, and the horse laughed, too, the way horses do.

"It's all a part of growing up, now that you are nine," chuckled Uncle Jacob as he closed the stable door. "Isn't that right, Chris?"

"Ja," grinned Christian.

# 2

# Covered-Wagon Days

"We are moving to Bavaria," announced Christian's father to his family one day.

"To Bavaria?" asked Christian. "But this is our home here in Weierhof, Father!"

Christian did not want to move away. He loved to watch the river run and the busy mill wheel turn. And he loved the big oak tree and his church on top of the hill.

He would miss running up and down the steps to his church. The big people always seemed to puff by the time they got to the top, but Christian thought that he could run up and down the steps all day if no one stopped him.

But then Christian remembered that his Uncle Jacob had already moved to Bavaria.

Leaving would be sad, but he would be glad to see Uncle Jacob and his horses again.

Christian thought of all these things while his father was talking. "Yes," said Father, "it is decided. We will also move to Bavaria as some of our relatives have done."

"Then it is settled," agreed Christian's mother as she cleared away the supper dishes on the table. "We all want to do what you think is best."

The days were extra busy now. Christian and his brothers helped their father get a big heavy wagon ready for the trip. The wagon had wide wheels and was to have a thatched roof.

First, Christian's father built the framework of a roof on the wagon and nailed a few boards across it the long way. Then he covered the boards with bundles of rye straw four inches deep.

"It will not matter if it rains," said Father as he put a rainproof cloth over the straw. "My family will be snug and dry." Father smiled at Christian and put his arm around him as they stood back to look at the wagon that was ready for its journey.

Mother checked the wagon with her head cocked to one side and her hands on her hips. "You did a good job," she praised him. "The covered wagon will be a nice home for us for a while."

On moving day as Christian looked at the church on the hill, a lump came into his throat. The lump got bigger as he thought of all of his good times in Weierhof.

"Giddap! Giddap!" Father shouted to the horses. Then he turned gaily to Mother. "We're off! You'll like it in Bavaria."

"And the rest of you will too," he said comfortingly as he looked at his family in the covered wagon.

There was a caravan of three wagons going to Bavaria. Two of Christian's uncles were going along.

The wagons jounced in and out of the German villages and around the edge of some of the towns. Sometimes they clattered over cobblestones. Other times they raised clouds of dust. Up the hills they went slowly, lumbering along.

The Krehbiels sang hymns inside their wagon. Or slept. Or talked. Or counted cows and geese. Or just looked. The countryside was like patchwork quilts, with tiny fields of green and gold colors.

One day Mother made up a song:

Oh, where will we go?
Oh, where, oh, where?
Does anyone know,
Does anyone care?

"You're like Uncle Jacob," laughed Christian. "He always makes up rhymes."
Then Father sang:

Oh, yes, I know just where we go.
And you will like it there.
It isn't far to our new home,
With a pull by the Krehbiel mare!

"You're like Uncle Jacob, too," shouted Christian, standing up in the wagon this time. "It will be good to see him again."
Everyone enjoyed Father's song. And they did have two fine mares pulling them to Bavaria.
"Sit down, Christian," warned Mother. "We want our family to arrive safely."
"That's right," agreed Father. "Indeed we do."

# 3

# Saying Good-bye

The caravan of wagons with its Krehbiel passengers arrived safely in Bavaria. It was wonderful to see Uncle Jacob again.

But soon Christian's father discovered that he could not do his farm work the same way he did it in Weierhof.

"Everything is different," he told his family one day. "Here in Bavaria the farmers do their threshing before the sun comes up, usually with at least six men. Back home in Weierhof, only two of us worked on the threshing floor until it was empty."

"It's different at school, too," added Christian. "Nothing is the same here."

"Well, we will soon feel at home," Mother encouraged them.

Once every two or three months, mail came from relatives in America. The letters told the Krehbiels that farmland in America was good and that people could do their work the way they felt was best.

While they lived in Bavaria for three years, Father sometimes thought about moving to America. Then one day it looked as though Jacob, Christian's oldest brother, would be drafted to join the German army.

Father announced, "We, too, must go to America. There we can practice peace instead of helping with wars. Jesus said we are to love our enemies, not kill them."

Mother looked at Father and then at the rest of her family. It would be hard to leave their nice farm and home, but she did not want her sons to grow up to be soldiers.

"It's all right," Mother told Father. "We will all go along. We want to obey God and do the things that are right. It is wonderful that the American government is kind to people who believe as we do."

It took months to get ready to go to America. It took so long that there was time for Christian to visit Weierhof once more.

He had fun climbing up the steps to the church on the hill and watching the mill wheel turn. And Christian was glad that he could sit again under the huge old oak tree with its wide branches that felt like arms keeping him safe.

"I won't ever forget you," Christian said to the old oak tree. "Or Weierhof either. Or Bavaria. I wonder what our new home is going to be like, don't you?"

The oak tree seemed to wonder, too, as its leaves whispered good-bye in Christian's ear. "I'll miss you, too," Christian thought the oak tree said.

After a while, the rest of Christian's family came to Weierhof to say good-bye to their relatives and friends. As the family looked at their old house and their church on the hill for the last time, they felt big lumps in their throats.

"Do you think our home in America will be as nice as this one?" wondered Christian with sadness in his voice.

"I'm sure God has a nice home waiting for us, Chris," said Mother. She smiled bravely as she gave him a hug. "We're moving to America because we want to obey God. We do not need to worry. God will take good care of us."

# Adventures at Sea

Down the Rhine River went a steamship with Christian and his family on it. Christian stood looking over the railing. Excitement tingled up and down his back, and his eyes did not miss a thing as the paddle wheel pushed the ship down the busy Rhine River.

Christian Krehbiel and his family were on their way to America. They had said good-bye to their relatives and friends in Bavaria and in Weierhof, Germany. Now they were chugging away on their journey downstream to the big shipping center of Rotterdam.

Christian watched the other boats pass the steamship. He looked at the pleasant villages and the fields of grapes going by. He knew that the grape farmers planted the rows of grapes in steps so that they could take care of their vines more easily.

He saw the merry clouds dancing along overhead. Sometimes they seemed to stop for a moment when Christian gazed at the castles perched high on the hills overlooking the river.

When the steamship came to Rotterdam, the Krehbiel family boarded another steamer on its way to France. The North Sea waters were rough, and the ship rocked hard.

Everyone was seasick. *I wish we had stayed in Germany,* Christian thought. But after the steward brought Christian something hot to drink, he felt better.

The people got off the steamer at Le Havre in France and boarded the *Splendid*, a ship with its prow facing toward America. The baggage had to be moved to that ship, too.

French stevedores treated the luggage roughly. One Frenchman, who wanted to be helpful, took a basket that belonged to the Krehbiel family and started to throw it on the piled-up baggage.

"Be careful!" shrieked Christian's mother. "That's our Peter!"

Peter was Christian's little brother. If Christian's mother had not stopped the man in time, Peter would have landed with a thud on the pile of boxes and trunks!

At last Christian heard someone shout, "All aboard! Sails up!"

Quickly the crew answered, "Heave ho!"

The anchor was raised, and the fast ship slid out into the Atlantic Ocean with the tide. Weierhof, with its mill and church and friendly *Hofs* (farms), was left behind.

Large fish called dolphins played near the ship. The sailors harpooned one of them.

One day a whale came to the surface of the white-capped water. Christian saw it spout water with its blast of breath. After taking in more air, the whale showed its long back and at last its tail before it disappeared under the white caps of the ocean again.

One Sunday the ship just floated on the ocean and the sails hung loose. Later, the wind blew. For several days Christian wondered if the ship would come out of the huge waves again whenever it nosedived.

The ship rocked high over one wave, suddenly plunged low into the trough, and then slammed into the next wave. Christian was glad the ship always came up

There in the distance was the long skyline of New York City!

again and rode the waves.

Once there was a hard storm. It came during the night while most of the people on the ship were sleeping. The gale tore at the sails and broke a crossbeam on the rigging.

All of the portholes were closed, so no water dashed through those little windows into the rooms of the passengers. Christian could hear the trunks bounce back and forth like toys in the hold at the bottom of the ship.

Excitement tingled up and down Christian's back again as the ship came closer to America. There in the distance was the long skyline of New York City! It looked like a drawing of colored lines against the sky.

It was 1851, and it had taken thirty-five days to reach the New York harbor in America. Christian and his family and the rest of the passengers were glad to step out on land again.

Christian was more eager than ever as he walked down the gangplank of the ship. The *Splendid* had been his home for five weeks.

Some of the people were almost dizzy as they tried their sea legs on the land. They discovered that walking around on a rocking ship is quite different from walking on ground that holds still.

But most of all, the travelers were thankful to God that they had arrived well and safe.

As he looked up at the tall dark buildings so close to him now, Christian thought he would like America. And he wondered what new adventures were waiting for him on the other side of those buildings that stood so high against the sky.

**5**

# The End of the Trip

The buildings in New York City loomed tall against the sky as Christian looked up. Nothing had ever looked so big and busy as that city.

But Christian and his family did not stay there long. They traveled up the Hudson River to Albany on a steamer and then by train along the Erie Canal to Buffalo. There they boarded a steamship for Cleveland, Ohio, where Christian's Uncle Daniel met the family.

Words tumbled over each other, and everyone wanted to talk at once. But Christian's father was anxious to get to work, and his mother could hardly wait to get settled again. The trip and caring for baby Peter had made her very tired.

When the travelers arrived at Hayesville, Ohio, it was late July. There was plenty of work to do right away with the harvest. Christian helped with threshing and worked hard stacking straw.

One day eighteen-year-old Christian noticed that the thermometer registered 100 degrees. "It's much hotter here than in Germany," he said to his father.

Christian wiped his sweating face on his big red handkerchief. "But I guess if everyone else can stand it, we can, too. *Gell, Vater?* (Isn't that right, Father?)"

"*Ja,*" agreed his father, laughing. "But let's have some lemonade. I'm really thirsty."

Christian's family did not stay in Ohio long because land there was expensive and some of it was still covered with forests.

That fall Christian and a friend named Henry left for Iowa, the state that would be their home. The rest of Christian's family planned to come in the spring when it was time to plant crops.

Christian and Henry felt like explorers as they went down the Ohio River and then up the Mississippi by riverboat. But the young men did not know much English, and it was hard to make people understand what they were trying to say.

At last Christian and Henry arrived in Keokuk, Iowa. "It certainly feels good to put our feet on the ground that will be our new home, doesn't it, Henry?" Christian asked. "Isn't Keokuk the name of an Indian chief?"

"I think so," answered Henry.

The boys found that though Keokuk was a small town, it was an important trading post.

Christian and Henry had to walk part of the way to Uncle Eymann's house. "I will be glad when we get there," sighed Christian as they tramped through the deep Iowa mud with their heavy baggage. "It can't be much farther."

"Well, I'm starved," declared Henry. "Chris, I hope your aunt has a good meal waiting for us."

Soon the boys heard Uncle Eymann's dog barking.

"Uncle Eymann's house at last!" shouted Christian joyfully.

Christian's aunt did have a good meal waiting for the boys. "Are you sure you have had enough?" she asked after the boys had eaten all they could hold. "You have made a long journey."

The boys were sure that they could not

eat another bite. They thanked her for preparing the food.

"What kind of work do you have for me?" Christian asked his Uncle Eymann.

"There are plenty of things for you to do, Chris," Uncle Eymann chuckled. "You may take care of the horses and cows and make fences for a while. Henry will help Uncle Miller Krehbiel."

So the days were busy again for Christian. Morning and evening he took care of the livestock on Uncle Eymann's farm. And there were always trees to chop down before he could make the rails for fences. Christian learned to be a good rail-splitter.

When spring came, Christian's family arrived from Ohio. Until their own house was ready, Christian and his family lived with neighbors.

Christian helped build their log house and log barn on the hundred acres his parents bought for $800. Each night Christian and his brother had to climb a ladder to the small attic room where they slept. After the weather turned cold, the boys laid a heavy wagon robe from Germany over their bed to keep them warm.

One night it snowed hard. The howling wind blew fine snow through the cracks of the house into their faces, but Christian and his brother pulled up the robe they brought from Germany and slept fine.

In the morning they found a foot of snow on their cover! Every night they crawled carefully under the blanket full of snow until the weather was warmer and the bedding could dry out. It was quite a trick to creep under the blanket without scattering the snow all around the room.

Often Christian wished he were home again in Germany in his own dry bedroom. But he knew why his father had decided to come to America. He knew why his father and mother left their fine farm home and took the expensive trip to a new land. It was because they did not want their six sons to be soldiers.

"I am glad Father wants to obey God," Christian told his brother one evening as they pulled the German blanket snugly up under their chins. "And I want to obey God, too.

"I am really thankful for America where we can live and work and do as Jesus taught us in the Bible. And soon we will have a warm house here, too, in America." Just then he went to sleep under the snow-topped cover.

● ● ●

At age twenty-five, Christian married Susanna Ruth and later moved to Illinois with her. They had sixteen children. For forty-five years he was a pastor and a key leader among the Mennonites of the Midwest. He worked with other interested people to start conferences, missions, and several schools and businesses.

Christian also helped Mennonites from Russia to settle in Kansas in the 1870s. When he was forty-seven years old, he moved his family to Kansas, was a pastor there, and did mission work with American Indians.

When he was a boy, Christian Krehbiel wanted to ride his black pony through the farmland of Weierhof. But he didn't know then how far he would travel in his lifetime!

•  •  •

Your parents and teachers may wish to read about Christian Krehbiel in *The Mennonite Encyclopedia*, volume 3 (Herald Press, 1957), or in his autobiography, *Prairie Pioneer* (Newton, Kansas: Faith and Life Press, 1969).

# PART THREE

# Pioneer
# Astronomer

# Contents

# 1

# The Stargazer

David Rittenhouse liked to study the stars best of all. Two hundred and fifty years ago, David lived in Norristown, not far from Germantown, Pennsylvania.

In spring and summer, when the green grass made a soft carpet for him, he watched the stars for hours.

"David!" Mother would call at last. "Come in now! Your clothes will be damp from the dew!"

Once more David looked at the Big Dipper, the Little Dipper, the North Star, Grandmother Cassiopeia in her rocking chair, and Orion the Hunter.

"I hope I can see you again tomorrow night!" he told his nighttime friends.

David pushed open the heavy door to their house built of fieldstones. He saw his father reading by candlelight. Mother sat in the rocker knitting, and his sisters, Margaret and Esther, were embroidering pillowcases.

"I wish I had a telescope so I could see the stars better," David said, brushing the grass off his shirt. "They are so far away!"

"Maybe you can build a telescope, David," Father suggested. "Study well, and perhaps you can do it. You like math and science, and you like to build things.

"I wish you could go to school, but there is no school near our home. You will have to read books on your own. I can help you with new words.

"If we lived in Germantown, you could have Christopher Dock for a teacher in the summers," Father added. "I have heard that he is a fine Mennonite schoolteacher and that he loves children."

"I wish I could go to school," David said, "but I am glad you can help me. I will study hard, and maybe God will show me how to make a telescope."

"But remember, David, I want you to be a farmer too," Father replied. "We have a lot of work right here on the farm. Our whole family needs to help."

Margaret and Esther, David's sisters, nodded their heads while they decorated the pillowcases. Their sewing needles made neat tiny stitches.

"I will help you with the farmwork, Father, but I can't keep the ideas from coming."

"You can think about them while you are plowing," Father said with a twinkle in his eye.

David's sisters did not always understand David and his dreams. They wondered about the stars, too, but didn't try to figure them out as their brother did.

David looked out the window at the stars once more. The boat-shaped moon was shining brightly.

"God seems near when I see the heavens at night," David whispered with feeling. Then he said his evening prayer on his knees in front of the window.

David thought for a while before he went to sleep. He clasped his hands together behind his dark brown head of hair. His soft gray eyes sparkled as he tried to understand the stars. He often dreamed during the night about making a telescope.

Years later Ann and Jane Taylor wrote a nursery rhyme about the stars for curious children like David:

Twinkle, twinkle, little star,
How I wonder what you are,
Up above the world so high,
Like a diamond in the sky!

For breakfast the next morning, David's mother served fried ham, warm bread and milk, and apple butter.

"Father," David asked, "why did Great-Grandfather William Rittenhouse come to America? Wasn't Germany a nice place to live?"

"Yes, Germany is a wonderful place to live, David. Crops grow well. Houses and cows and sheep dot the beautiful countryside. Families enjoy going to town with their horses and wagons and visiting the big cities.

"They like to take walks in the woods on Sunday afternoons. There are bouquets of violets to pick in the spring. The Rhine River in Germany is wide and busy with many boats."

"Then why did Great-Grandfather move to America?"

"The government did not allow people to worship God the way they felt was right," Father replied.

"They could not think their own thoughts or pray their own prayers. The rulers wanted to control everything."

"There were many wars. The government tried to take young men to fight, but Great-Grandfather believed in peacemaking. And in those wars, farms were ruined and people were killed."

"I'm glad Great-Grandfather moved to America," David said. "It's safer here. I want to keep on thinking my own thoughts and praying my own prayers. I want to dream dreams about building a telescope someday."

After they had eaten their breakfast, Father led in a prayer of thanks for the meal. He even talked about David as he prayed.

"Dear heavenly Father, be with David while he grows up. If you have a special job for him to do, please help him to get ready for it and to study well. Guide all of us and give us strength to do the work you want us to do. Amen."

# 2

# A Trip to Germantown

The next day was Friday. David wanted to watch the men work at Great-Grandfather's paper mill along Paper Mill Run. The Indians called it the Monoshone Creek, a branch of the Wissahickon Creek.

Grandfather Nicholas had also worked at this paper mill. Father needed some paper, so he took David along to Germantown.

David hoped there would be time to go fishing in the creeks.

"Try to catch a couple of catfish," Mother called.

"We will try!" David called back loudly as the wagon jounced down the lane.

As they rode along, Father explained that paper was needed by everyone. He said that Great-Grandfather William Rittenhouse had made paper when he lived in Germany. When he moved to Amsterdam, he called himself a papermaker.

Soon after he arrived in America, he started building a paper mill near Germantown. This was the first paper mill in America. David could not study nearly as well if there were no paper for books and notes.

After a while, they came to the mill and went in to look around. The great rollers turned out big rolls of white paper. Linen rags were best to make paper. First the scraps were soaked in water for two months.

Then a wooden hammer pounded the rags into pulp. The clean flowing water in Paper Mill Run drove the waterwheel which kept the hammer moving. David came as close as he could without being in the way of the workers.

The sounds, smells, and activity at the mill interested David. He noticed how all the wheels and cogs and belts pulled together to bring power from the waterwheel to help do the work at many places.

Each man had his part in the whole job of making paper. Some were stooped and their large hands were red from reaching in the cold water every workday for years.

A sign on the wall said that William Bradford, the first printer in Pennsylvania, used the well-made paper from the Rittenhouse mill.

As they looked around, Father told David that Great-Grandfather's paper mill also had made paper for the first newspaper printed in New York. The first Mennonite book made in America was printed with Great-Grandfather's paper.

Then Father had business to do, so David and Jacob, a friend of his who lived near the paper mill, went fishing. They looked for worms and grasshoppers and headed for Wissahickon Creek.

"Mother said a fish dinner would taste good with potatoes and dandelion greens," David told Jacob.

"I hope the fish bite good today," Jacob said. "My mother wants fish for dinner, too."

The warm summer sun felt good on their backs, and they stuck their feet in the water. The trees with the light green leaves were all around them and gave them shade.

"I like spring and summer," David said. "It's a quiet time and we can think about things."

David and Jacob went fishing in the Wissahickon
Creek.

"I know," said Jacob. "I keep thinking of working in the paper mill when I grow up. I already help there once in a while. I guess some of us need to be farmers, but there are other kinds of jobs."

"I want to build a telescope," David told Jacob, "so I can see the stars better."

But Jacob didn't ask about that because right then he felt a tug on his fishing line.

"I've got a bite!" he squealed. He pulled hard on his pole and flipped a fish out of the water. "What a big one! Look, it's a catfish!"

David was excited. "It's my turn," he said. Before long he had a catfish on the end of his line, too.

The boys fished for several hours and each one had a nice string of fish to take home. They caught more catfish, a trout, a bass, and some sunfish. The sunfish were the colors of a rainbow.

"Does your mother fry the sunfish, bones and all?" asked David.

"Yes," said Jacob. "They taste best that way. I like them crispy."

Father helped to clean their fish when he and David got home. "Good catch, David!" Father said. "These fish will taste delicious for supper."

Mother praised David too. "You and Jacob are true-blooded fishermen," she said proudly.

David looked shyly down at his plate. He wasn't used to receiving so much praise, but he was glad about the big catch.

# 3

# Time for Meeting

Grandmother Rittenhouse invited David's family to spend Saturday and Sunday with them in late fall. They would ride to the Germantown meetinghouse for worship on Sunday. There Great-Grandfather had been the first Mennonite preacher for the first Mennonite congregation in America.

Grandfather Nicholas Rittenhouse had also preached there, but he had died when David was two years old. So Grandmother was lonely and loved to have her family come and visit her.

The air was crisp and cool. "It feels like snow is just around the corner," Father said, noticing a few rustling leaves on the almost-bare trees. "We must get an early start and wear our warmest clothes."

"Why are some people called Mennonites?" asked David on the way to the meeting. Next to studying stars, he liked questions and answers best.

The horses pranced as Father slapped the reins. Now that they lived on the farm in Montgomery County, it was about fifteen miles to Germantown.

"Mennonites had their beginning in Europe about 200 years ago," Father explained.

Then he told David that the word *Mennonite* came from the name of Menno Simons. This man became a key leader among the early Anabaptists in Holland.

He had been a priest in another church before he joined the Anabaptists. As he studied the Bible, he came to the same faith in Christ that the Anabaptists had.

They believed they should not baptize babies, but only baptize people old enough to want to be baptized.

Baptized members needed to understand what it meant when they said they trusted Christ to save them. They would promise to care for each other in the church and to follow the way of Jesus as long as they lived.

Father also told David that Mennonites believe in living a simple life, obeying God's rules, and loving everybody.

"They don't help to kill people during a war, and they try to be friends with everyone.

"Some people treat their slaves badly," Father went on. "They beat them more than their animals. Some slaves have scars all over their bodies."

"That's not kind," said David. "Can't anyone do anything about it?"

"We hope so, David. Some Mennonites and Quakers want to sign their names to a letter to the government against keeping slaves. Perhaps that will help.

"We think slaves should be set free. At least owners of slaves should treat them as fairly as they themselves want to be treated."

David ran up the steps two at a time to the small plain-looking log meetinghouse on top of the hill. Soon everyone joined in singing the hymns.

David smiled when Deacon Jansen read from the Bible, Psalm 19:

How clearly the sky reveals God's glory!
How plainly it shows what he has done!

Then the beloved Bishop Jacob Gottschalk preached that morning about the beauty and greatness of God's world. As he spoke, he quoted from Psalm 8:

When I look at the sky,
    which you have made,
    at the moon and the stars,
    which you set in their places—
what is man, that you think of him;
    mere man, that you care for him?

The old bishop looked toward the ceiling as though he were gazing at the sky. A verse from Psalm 147 came to his mind, and he recited it:

He has decided the number of the stars
    and calls each one by name.

"Can you believe those verses about the stars?" David whispered to his father. "That God can count the stars, millions of them, and has given each one a name? God is the greatest one in the whole world!"

Father put his hand on David's knee. "I hope you will always remember God's greatness," he said quietly.

While Grandmother Rittenhouse and

David's mother and sisters made dinner, Father took the old family Bible and showed David the verses about stars. David read them over and over. He wanted to say them often so he would not forget them.

The dinner at Grandmother's table was delicious. There was roast chicken and gravy, mashed potatoes, corn, cranberries, applesauce, and molasses cookies.

Snow had started falling during the worship service, and by early afternoon it was several inches deep.

So David asked, "Do we have time for a sled ride? The hills around here are perfect for sledding."

"Sure," Father said, "take a few rides. I'll come out and watch you and the girls sled while the women do the dishes. You need to use up some energy anyway before the long trip home."

David wished he could go sledding forever. The crisp air and the clean white snow made a beautiful world, just as the bishop said. David liked the way his cold cheeks felt in the nippy air.

The children came back in the house to warm up and dry off before the trip home. Grandmother heated some bricks to put in the wagon for foot warmers. Then she tucked warm blankets around everyone.

"Thank you for a good time!" shouted David's family as the wagon pulled away. Its wheels were cutting through the soft drifting snow. Grandmother watched as long as she could and enjoyed the song of the jingling bells on the frisky horses.

# 4

# Stories for David

The months went by and soon it was spring. When the ground dried out enough, the farmers began to prepare the land for the growing season.

One sunny morning David and his father were out plowing a field. They wanted to plant oats as early as possible. David was riding the lead horse to keep it going straight.

While they rested their horses for a few minutes, David said, "I was born here on April 8 in 1732. Sometimes I wonder when the first Mennonites came to America. Can you tell me, Father?"

"Let's see," said Father, pulling at his beard. "In the 1650s, some Dutch Mennonites were living here and there in New Amsterdam, later renamed New York City. But there were no Mennonite congregations.

"By 1663 Mennonite settlers came to Delaware for freedom to worship God in their own way and to share their belongings. They didn't fight or have slaves. But a year later their village was run over by war between the Dutch and the British. The people were scattered.

"Then the ship *Concord* brought Dutch-speaking Mennonites and Quakers from Krefeld, Germany, near Holland. They arrived at Penn's Landing in Philadelphia on October 6, 1683, about sixty years ago.

"They had to hike for six miles to Germantown, carrying some of their things with them. Germantown is the first Mennonite settlement in America that lasted.

"The new settlers were all linen weavers. The fall colors must have been on the leaves then. There were thirteen families, and they built their homes along an old Indian trail in Germantown. But they had to work fast because the first snow was not far away.

"They were thankful for all the trees they could use to build their homes and to burn in their fireplaces. Some people lived in caves. The first winter was desperately cold and full of snow, but the children had fun sledding."

"That's for sure," David said, remembering his sled rides on the hills near Grandmother's house.

"Now let's make another round with the plow and give the sea gulls more worms to eat," said Father.

When they stopped to rest, David asked what happened next in the new settlement.

"After a while some Mennonites moved to Germantown from New York, and about sixteen more families came from Europe between 1683 and 1703," David's father went on. "The first Mennonites here spoke Dutch, but most of those who came later were from Germany or Switzerland and spoke German.

"Great-Grandfather came to America in 1688. He was born in Germany and later moved to Holland. He could speak German and Dutch, and he learned English too.

"Great-Grandfather Rittenhouse began building a paper mill right away. He chose the spot where the present mill is, the one we visited. His son Gerret built a flour mill on Chisholm Creek.

"How do you think Great-Grandfather

felt when the mill he built was carried away by the flood?" David wondered.

"He couldn't believe it, I'm sure," replied Father. "One day the mill stood by Paper Mill Run near the Wissahickon Creek, and the next day it had floated away. The mill, the waterwheel, machines, rolls of paper, piles of rags, tools, and other things were lost.

"William Penn, a Quaker from England who founded Pennsylvania, asked people to help rebuild the mill. *Pennsylvania* means Penn's Woods. It was named in honor of Penn's father, Sir William Penn.

" 'Pray for courage for the Rittenhouses,' Penn said. People listened to him, and soon there was a new paper mill. He even gave some money of his own to help.

"William Penn wanted the Indians and all the people to be treated gently and to learn the Christian faith. The Quakers from England were the first settlers, and then the Dutch and Germans came.

"As more and more Mennonites arrived, they spread into the country to the north-west along Skippack Creek, where Christopher Dock lives. Then some went farther west to the Lancaster area."

The horses pawed at the ground and snorted, so Father took them on another round of plowing. When they got back to the end of the field, David wanted to hear more. So Father wiped his forehead and sat on the stone fence beside David.

"Great-Grandfather William Rittenhouse was the first Mennonite minister in America. The people met in homes until a log meetinghouse was built in 1708. That was the year Great-Grandfather died."

"Father, tell me that story again, about Great-Grandfather and the blind man."

"Well, in 1695 Great-Grandfather found a man and a woman wandering around in Germantown. They were old and their clothes were dirty and torn. Because they hadn't eaten well for a long time, they were thin, weak, and sick.

"The man was a Mennonite preacher named Plockhoy from Delaware. Thirty-one years earlier, the people in his village had been driven away and robbed by soldiers.

"Great-Grandfather took care of Plockhoy and his wife. He called on members of his church to raise some money to build them a little house. The man was blind. The Plockhoys were grateful for everyone's kindness. As long as they lived, they felt at home with the Germantown Mennonites."

Then Father took the horses on another

round of plowing while David went to the barn to tend the animals. Soon Father returned. When they finished their chores, they went to the house with a bucket of milk from their cow.

After supper David talked with his mother while she was knitting a sweater for Father.

"Let's make a list of the kinds of work the pioneers did," David suggested, "besides farming and papermaking."

"You have a million questions in your head, don't you, David?" Mother smiled as her knitting needles kept up a steady *click-click*.

David named a few kinds of work like printing and spinning and bookmaking. Mother thought of those who make baskets from rye straw, weavers, makers of iron kettles and pots and pans, and builders of Dutch ovens.

"Some pioneers knitted clothes, and others made shoes," she added.

"Did anyone want to build a telescope?"

"I don't know of anyone. Maybe that's going to be your job."

"We made quite a list," David said as he went over to their oven and the small boiler his mother used over hot coals.

Then David noticed the toaster and the

waffle iron. With their handles, each was four feet long. And there was the sandstone sink with the stopper. The water ran in a pipe through the wall and right out on the ground.

Some of their dishes were made of clay. David also checked the candles Mother made from animal fat or beeswax. She molded them or dipped them. She needed to make a lot because he and Father liked to read so much in the evenings.

The candles reminded David that he wanted to read some more before it was time for bed. Mother's candlelight helped him to see just fine. When he came to a word he didn't know, he asked his father or mother for help.

When he went to bed in the attic, David said the Bible verses about the stars over and over. Through the window the North Star shone brightly that night.

David still wondered how God could think up millions of names for the stars. Perhaps he used names from all the languages in the world. He wished he could talk to God about it.

**5**

# Flowers for Mother

The next morning David was eating a piece of pie dough shaped like a pretzel. "Mother," he asked, "do you know where Menno Simons wrote his books?"

"He wrote them under a linden tree in front of his house in northern Germany. He wrote that we should be happy with just the little things," Mother replied. "Menno also wanted us to remember the rules God taught and to love everyone."

"Yesterday Father told me about Mennonites coming to America, but we didn't have time to talk much about Menno Simons. What does a linden tree look like?"

"It has sweet-smelling flowers, David. Menno Simons liked to be outdoors as much as he could."

"That gives me an idea. Perhaps I can find some spring flowers for you."

Mother smiled. "I would like that," she said joyfully. "Bouquets of God's flowers show God's love, and yours too."

David hurried down the street and climbed the hill to the woods. How good everything smelled! The new leaves were on all the trees, the birch, elm, oak, maple, walnut, and hickory. The beautiful evergreens kept their color all year.

David smiled broadly when he saw the violets, the spring beauties, and the stars of Bethlehem. They were lovely with their lavender and pink and white colors.

"And there are the yellow dogtooth violets!" David announced to his friends in the woods. Squirrels and rabbits showed themselves, and in the distance he could even see some deer grazing.

Near a little stream, David found some jack-in-the-pulpit flowers. They were David's favorite. Each looked like a little man preaching from his pulpit just like their minister on Sunday.

David rested against a dogwood tree for a while and watched the animals at play. The squirrels were chasing each other, leaping here and there in the branches.

They held their paws so gracefully when they found a nut or acorn to eat.

A rabbit streaked by in the brush, but David saw only his cottontail. Some of the birds flew in a straight line; others, like the junco, swooped up and down.

David decided that the animals must have had breakfast early this morning. The birds were busy saying thank-you. Besides juncos, David saw wood doves, bluejays, cardinals, wood thrushes, and sparrows.

"I am going to bring you some cracked seeds next time I come," David promised.

"I love it here in the woods. Penn's Woods is a good name for this piece of land, so we'll call it Pennsylvania." He was talking to all of his animal friends.

Then David broke off some twigs with dogwood blossoms to add to his handful of flowers. When he came home, Mother liked her bouquet. She wiped her hands on her apron and found a vase in the cupboard for the flowers.

"Thank you, David," she said, smiling gratefully. "Now I feel like I too have had a walk in the woods already this morning. The flowers make the house look lovely and smell delightful."

"Next to stars and questions, I like the woods best," David told his mother. "The stars and the woods give time for quiet thoughts. They give me time to dream. I wish I could plan how to build a telescope."

"You will," Mother promised David. "If you reach for the stars, I am sure you can build a telescope to see them better."

# 6

# The Treasure Chest

One morning Father said, "Let's get busy, David. We're going to do some plowing in the upper field. It's almost time to plant corn."

The slender boy with the soft gray eyes said, "All right, Father."

But David's thoughts were busy, just as busy as his father's. As he rode the lead horse, he worked out some ideas in his mind.

David wanted to make a small water-wheel like the one at Great-Grandfather's paper mill near the Wissahickon Creek. That evening he took a pencil and some paper and drew a plan for it.

By afternoon of the next day, Father and

David had the field plowed, and David had tested his plans in his mind. That evening he made a few changes to his drawing.

When morning came, he gathered wood and used his father's tools to make the model waterwheel. It took him two days to shape the pieces and put them together.

Then with stones, clay, and twigs, he made a little dam to hold back the tiny stream running from their spring. While the water filled up behind the dam, David placed his waterwheel a few feet below it.

Next he used boards to prepare a trough that carried the water to the top of his waterwheel. And the wheel worked!

David put the tools away and called his family to see his waterwheel spinning. Whenever neighbors stopped to visit, David showed them his waterwheel. They could hardly believe that a young boy, only eight years old, had done such a hard thing!

A few years later David learned that when his Uncle David died, he had left a chest of carpenter tools and a few books on mathematics. Twelve-year-old David had discovered a real treasure chest!

No one else wanted such old things. It was David's very own chest, and the things inside were precious and valuable and belonged to him.

David made a little dam to hold back the stream and supply water to run his waterwheel.

In the evenings David drew plans on a slate or on paper. As he worked, he often stopped to write math problems and make sketches with chalk. David plowed, harrowed, sowed seeds, and harvested crops like other farm boys. But his mind was busy with other things at the same time.

He wrote on his plow handles and on the fences around the fields. David thought of moving cogs and levers and numbers all the time.

"David!" called Benjamin, his younger brother. "Mother says it's time for dinner!"

Benjamin saw the numbers and pictures David had drawn on the plow beam and handles.

As they walked slowly back to the house together, Benjamin laughed and said, "I think you like math and science better than food."

Benjamin could not understand that. He was always ready to eat.

When David was seventeen, he made a wooden clock. After this he made a metal clock. But he kept right on drawing plans for building a telescope.

David's father wanted him to be a farmer, but he saw that this was not going to happen. He gave his son money to buy some tools he needed in Philadelphia.

David built a shop by the roadside and made clocks and instruments to sell. He also mended clocks that were broken or had stopped running. When he had free time, he worked on his telescope.

David liked what he was doing so much that he almost lost track of time for himself. He worked during the day and studied at night. One winter he became sick, and a cold in his lungs hung on for a long time. He had to cough and cough until he was better.

Friends were giving him books, and David kept on learning more and more about the sky. He would read by candlelight until it was late because he wanted to learn everything he could about the stars.

# 7

# Finished at Last!

In a room upstairs in his town house in Philadelphia, David had his own observatory. He built his telescope there and finished it at last!

People said David was the first person in America to make a telescope. He was also the first scientist to use threads from spiderwebs to make the cross hairs for it. With his telescope, he could see east and west for nearly fifty miles, and much farther in the sky at night.

David was married by now and had two daughters, Elizabeth and Esther. They enjoyed looking at the stars through the telescope just as much as their mother did. The sky seemed much closer.

"Your dream has really come true, Papa," Elizabeth said happily, dancing in a circle around him.

"Do you see the four moons of Jupiter?" her father asked.

"I see them!" shouted Esther.

Elizabeth noticed the mountains and the great plains on the moon.

Through the telescope Father showed his family some of the faint stars that they had never been able to see before.

Benjamin Franklin, a well-known leader, often came to David's observatory to study the stars and electricity. Other great mathematicians and scientists worked with David, too.

David made a model of the way the planets turn around the sun and how they make paths in the sky. He used brass and ivory for the sun, and brass for the planets and moons. Wheelwork moved the balls to show how those bodies relate in the solar system.

People called David's model an orrery, and it is on display at the Franklin Institute in Philadelphia. Look for one like it when your family or your school group goes on a field trip to a science center or a planetarium.

David prepared such models for Princeton College in New Jersey and for the University of Pennsylvania in Philadelphia.

The second president of the United States, John Adams, said that David's models were most beautiful. They copied the motions of the planets, the sun, and the moon. People did not know of any other models like David's. Students could watch and figure out how far these bodies were from each other.

David also made instruments for surveying and helped to mark the borders between states such as Delaware and Pennsylvania. This was the first part of what was later called the Mason-Dixon line, between states of the North and the South.

Eclipses interested David. These happen when one heavenly body blocks some of the light from another one. Sometimes the moon moves between us and the sun, making the sun darker and casting a shadow on the Earth. That is a solar eclipse.

Other times Earth may move between the sun and the moon, making a shadow on the moon. That is called a lunar eclipse. A stellar eclipse happens when light from a star is blocked.

In a minute David could tell just where there was an eclipse in the past 5000 years and when there would be one in the 5000 years to come.

The observatory which David Rittenhouse built in 1769 at Norristown helped scientists figure the distance from Earth to the sun and to other stars.

As David looked through his telescope one night, he discovered that there were gases and air around Venus, one of the planets.

David wished he knew more about the Milky Way. There were millions of small stars in a band of light in the sky. He could hardly believe that God knew each one by name.

Thomas Jefferson, the third president of the United States, said good things about David. He had not made a world, the president stated. But because of his carefully built models of heavenly bodies, he had come closer to the Creator God than any other person.

A number of years later when David was quite sick, he told a friend, "You helped to make the way to God easier."

The friends clasped hands with each other. "You did too," his friend said. "Now many people can see the stars and planets better, and we are all closer to God."

David was tired, but happy. "I want everyone to know God better," he said. "That's why I worked so hard to make a telescope and all kinds of instruments."

David's friend pushed the curtain aside at the window. There was a soft glow from the moon and the stars. It warmed the room with God's love.

David smiled again. He was content. His dream had come true.

He was thankful that Pennsylvania was such a great place to live. William Penn knew that everyone needed time to think their own thoughts, as they chose to think. People wanted a place where they would be safe and free to dream dreams and to pray to God in their own church.

David, a tall slender man, talked softly to his friend. He felt sad because the black people were treated so badly, and he wanted the Conestoga Indians to have the things they needed.

David liked simple things, and he wanted to share what he had. He treated his neighbors kindly and loved pets and children. He was happy that he had two girls of his own.

David was guided by an old story. In the beautiful, stone 1770 Mennonite meeting-house in Germantown there is a famous table. Through the years, word has been passed along that on that very table a paper was signed in 1688 by four German settlers to help free the slaves.

"All men shall be free here in America," they declared.

After his friend left, David was alone but felt that God was present. "I'm glad I could help people find you through your wonderful creation," he prayed to God.

"And thank you for making my dreams come true. I know that wherever I am, I will appreciate the stars you have made most of all."

David walked over to the window in his bedroom. He prayed one more prayer with the starlight and moonlight shining in. "How great you are, O God," he said, bowing his head. "Only you can light a star."

● ● ●

In encyclopedias you may find more facts about David Rittenhouse, astronomer, inventor, clockmaker, and mathematician.

# PART FOUR

# Music of
# the Farm

# Contents

# 1

# Sook, Boss! So-o-k!

Home for Henry was on a prairie farm near Metamora, Illinois, about one hundred years ago. He loved his farm home and his family, and golden days followed one after another.

In the evening small Henry walked with big steps from the farmhouse to the front gate. He was on his way to the barnyard to call the cows. It was milking time.

"Sook, Boss!" he called. "So-o-k, Boss!"

"Sook, Boss! So-o-k!" Henry heard Father calling the cows, too. He ran to Father.

"Want to stroke Bessy?" Father asked. Henry said he did, so Father lifted him high in the air. He could look right into Bessy's gentle eyes.

"It's milking time now," Henry told Bessy, with his mouth at her ear. "You can eat some sweet grass again tomorrow."

The air was full of the music of "Sook, Boss" as Father and Henry herded the cows. Bessy took the lead and followed the narrow, winding path from the pasture into the milking pen.

The cows seemed glad to go. After all, they had important work to do. Henry's family needed milk to drink for supper.

The busy barn was a friendly place at milking time, but Henry liked the outdoors better.

Outside everything sang: the frogs in the mud, the birds from the treetops, the wind rustling the big leaves of the cottonwoods and sighing through the pines.

Most of all, Henry loved to play under the giant cottonwood trees and the tall willows that grew all about the barnyard and the cow pasture. He liked to hear the trees whispering secrets to each other.

Henry also listened for the cheery evening whistle of the bobwhite from the apple tree near the house.

And Father's work songs made him happy: "Hee-o-hee," and "Sook, Boss! So-o-o-k!"

Not far from the barn was a pasture

where the tall wild grass grew. "Buffalo used to feed here," Father told Henry one day. "See the part of the pasture that is so wet? That is called a slough. Snakes and frogs like to live there."

"I like to hear the frogs sing at night," said Henry.

"I do, too," Father agreed. "They sing their croaking song over and over, and it helps us all to go to sleep."

Henry did not know who could sing the best, the birds, frogs, trees, meadows, or Father. But probably it was Father.

# 2

# The New Coat

One day toward the end of summer, Henry did not feel well. His head was hot, as hot as the scorching day outdoors.

"Henry has *diphtheria*," he heard Mother saying in a troubled voice.

For weeks Henry was hot and sick. Everyone was sad and worried. Would Henry get well? They didn't know.

But one lovely day he woke up and the terrible fever was gone.

"You can get out of bed today, Henry," Mother said in her smiling voice. She helped her youngest son out of bed.

Henry's legs were wobbly from having fever and being in bed so long. But he used the wall to steady himself and walked to the living room. There he found a surprise waiting for him. It was a brand new coat!

Mother helped him put it on, and it was just his size.

"You do not need the coat yet," Mother told Henry, "but we wanted to buy it for you now to help celebrate. We are so glad you are going to get well."

Mother wiped some tears of happiness away with the corner of her apron. She and Father both knew that Henry had been very, very ill.

"Thank you for my new coat," Henry said happily. All of his brothers were smiling, too, and his baby sister, Katie, kicked extra hard in her little bed.

That evening at family prayers, Father thanked God for making Henry well.

# 3

# Time for School

It was the first day of school for Henry. His mother was packing the lunch kettles.

"I think I have put enough lunch in your dinner pail for two hungry boys!" she told Henry with a smile. "Sam, you be sure to see that Henry has an apple at recess. He'll be hungry from his new adventure."

"I will," promised Sam.

Mother seemed almost as excited about school starting as Henry was.

Instead of a tablet, Henry had a slate, a small wood-framed chalkboard for one person. In his book bag he also carried some brightly colored slate pencils and a yellow book called a primer, which was a beginner's reading book.

"Have a nice day!" Mother and Father called out as the boys walked down the lane.

Henry learned many of the same things children learn in school today. As he grew older, he liked geography and history and poems the best.

One day Henry's teacher, Miss Amanda Martin, said, "The Earth is not flat. It is round. The land and sky do not really meet in the distance. They only seem to come together. We call that meeting place the horizon."

Henry thought and thought about what Miss Martin said. The Earth seemed flat to him. He daydreamed that if he wanted to, he could jump off where the land and sky seem to meet.

Henry had also thought the stars God made were as big as a wagon, but the geography books said they were larger than the Earth itself. These were new ideas for Henry, and he turned them over in his mind for a long time.

The years passed, and finally Henry was finishing grade school. On the last day, everyone came to school early for the picnic.

Today there was a lot of free time outdoors. The children played some special games like town ball and needle's eye.

At noon, dinner looked and smelled wonderful. A white tablecloth covered the table, and on it were chicken, beef, ham, pickled red beet eggs, potato salad, cheese, pickles, oranges, apples, cakes of different colors, peach and strawberry jams, and lots more.

For dessert there were also delicious pumpkin, cherry, and custard pies. What a grand school picnic it was!

Henry and his friends sat under the shade of the maples. "What will it be like not to come back to school next year?" they wondered.

In the afternoon, everyone sang hymns and there was a program. Henry had a debate with his cousin, Joe. It was a funny subject, "Resolved: That the shotgun is more useful on the farm than the cow." Henry spoke for the statement, and Joe against it.

The next fall a wonderful thing happened for Henry. A new teacher came to the school, and Father said he would let Henry return to school for extra study after the fall work was done.

September, October, and November came and went. Henry could hardly wait to begin. Then one day in December, Father said at last, "Well, Henry, I guess you may start to school today."

The new teacher helped Henry to like books. At the end of the first day with Willie Whitmore, Henry took a book home to study. He had never done that before!

Each weekend Henry could hardly wait for Monday so he could go to school again. Every day was exciting because the new teacher made everything so interesting.

The first book he really loved to read listed titles of other books on its back cover: *Rip van Winkle*, *Robinson Crusoe*, and *Sinbad the Sailor*.

The ad said these books cost just a few pennies each. For a quarter Henry could buy enough books to read for the whole winter.

Henry ordered the books, and how happy he was when they came in the mail! When Henry was a boy, homes and schools did not have many books.

The stories stirred Henry's interest in the things he read about—the sea, Indian summer, the prairie, and railroads. Henry liked to travel these *story* roads to faraway places. Some day he hoped he could really go and see them for himself.

Once he read a book called *The Red Headed Family*. It made him want to learn the names and habits of birds. Henry invited his cousin Joe to help him look for a thrush's nest one Saturday morning.

"Maybe we can see the eggs of the blackbird, too, and the tiny family of the yellowhammer in the big cottonwood," he said.

During his time with the new teacher, Henry decided to become a schoolteacher himself.

"You'll make a good teacher, Henry," Willie Whitmore said to him. "I know you will."

None of Henry's relatives were teachers, and none of the Mennonites near Metamora were teachers, either.

More than anything else, Henry wanted to be a good teacher like Willie Whitmore. He knew he would try hard to make his dream come true.

# 4

# Sorting the Mail

Back of the Smith farm ran a small stream. Willow trees grew along the banks, and Sam and Johnie and Henry spent many pleasant hours building model dams to turn waterwheels.

Often they fished for minnows. They used worms for bait and fishhooks they had made themselves.

Each fall Henry and his family gathered walnuts from the row of tall trees that grew in the old orchard. All kinds of apple trees grew there, too.

Henry liked to eat the apple pies his mother baked. In the evenings when he was not too sleepy, he would eat an apple while he looked through the Montgomery

Ward catalog or played dominoes with his brothers.

Henry also enjoyed looking through the catalog from a jewelry firm in New York by the name of John Lynn and Company. For a little money, people could buy solid gold watch chains and cuff buttons.

Henry did not buy much, but he looked at the catalogs again and again.

Some papers came in the mail advertising free things, such as samples of corn cures. There were sewing machines for ninety-three dollars. Henry sent in ten cents to have his name put on the mailing list for free things.

For over a year, most of the mail in the Smith mailbox was addressed to Henry. Every Saturday the family went to town, and their mailbox at the post office was always full. Henry thought it was fun to sort the mail and look for his name on letters.

# 5

# A Race

Sometimes Henry played with the Cook boys who lived across the road from Cousin Ben's house. One time some of Henry's cousins and the neighbor Cook boys were building a model engine and thresher with smokestack, wheels, stacker, and everything.

They were making it of wood and would run it with a crank instead of steam. The boys needed Henry's two small wagon wheels to complete the engine.

"Would you sell your wheels for a fishhook and my pocketknife?" asked Henry Cook.

"*Nein*," said Henry. "I want to keep them."

The Cook boy decided to take them anyway. He and some other boys came down to Henry's house and picked up the wheels and walked home.

Henry had a plan. He was going to get those wheels back. They were valuable to him.

A few days later he found the three boys busy at work near the old shop on the Cook farm. They were putting their engine together, but they had not yet used the wheels. Henry saw them lying about ten feet away from the boys.

Henry started talking to the boys. While they were busy with their engine, he quickly picked up the wheels and ran home as fast as his legs could carry him.

The boys noticed that Henry had stopped talking. Then they looked up and saw Henry far down the road.

"We can catch him!" shouted Henry Cook. "He's younger than we are. Come on, let's go!"

Henry was in the lead, but three larger fellows were after him. He heard the patter of their bare feet behind him, but did not dare look back. For a while the pattering seemed to come nearer.

Then two of the boys gave up the race. About halfway between the Cook home

Henry was in the lead, but three larger fellows were after him.

and Henry Smith's house, Henry Cook seemed to be dropping back. When Henry Smith reached the bridge not far from his front gate, Henry Cook gave up, too.

Henry did not stop running until he had reached the barnyard. He threw himself on the grass. The sweat was running down his face. When he looked up, he saw Henry Cook just beyond the bridge making faces at him.

But he felt happy, knowing that he had outrun the other Henry. Later, the wheels were a part of his own engine.

Henry dreamed about tools and machines that would save people work, like an oat shucker and a corn shucker. He wanted to place a lever at the door of the barn that would make the grain and hay fall into the feeding troughs of the horses.

He planned for a lever which he could pull to take the harness off the backs of the horses. Now we push buttons, but during the age of steam machines, levers were pulled to start things.

Father's shop was stocked with tools and wheels and parts of broken machinery. Henry liked to work there to make things that he saw on the farm or at medicine shows and the county fair.

At different times he made a hayrack, a

threshing machine, some juggler's tools, and a whistle. Once, after watching a juggler perform, Henry taught himself to toss three balls into the air and keep them all going without dropping a single one.

Each year old blind Peter, the peddler, drove his horse and wagon around with things to sell. He often stayed overnight at the Smith home.

One evening Henry's father and mother were visiting with Pete, and Henry could hear what they were saying. His parents said they thought Henry would be a carpenter because he liked woodworking tools so much. Henry wondered if that would come true.

**6**

# Harvesting Oats

For Henry, the work on the farm made music. The farm machines had their own busy songs to sing, and Henry liked the sounds.

The hardest, hottest work was harvesting oats. Nothing mattered during those late-July and early-August days except getting the oats cut.

Everyone in the family helped. Even Rover, the big Newfoundland dog, was extra busy chasing rabbits through the oats.

"Time to take lunch out to the men!" Henry's mother would say. Henry ran toward the house when she called. The lunch basket and water jug were heavy.

The men took short stops to drink, oil

*136*

the binder, supply it with binder twine, and give the horses a rest. At lunch they took a longer break, but then they went right back to work.

It was a race against time. They wanted to finish the harvest before it rained or the oats fell to the ground. A big part of their living was from the harvest, and the weather was important to all the farmers.

Sometimes Henry's job was to ride Flora, the lead horse, along the edge of the standing oats and keep her from eating too much. Flora liked the crisp oat kernels.

She and four other horses were attached to the heavy binder made of wood and cast-iron. Henry was supposed to guide the lead team straight and help the whole rig turn the corners.

In the mornings, Henry felt good doing this. His job was important, and the air was cool and pleasant. In the hot afternoons, he was glad when the last field of oats had been cut for the day. His legs burned from rubbing against the sweaty body of Flora.

When the big green bottle flies bothered the horses, they kicked and bit and swished their tails to chase them away. Then Henry had to hold tightly to Flora and the reins.

All day long, Henry heard the steady rattle of the sickle bar. The draper chains rippled as they circled over the sprocket wheels. He heard the click of the binder arm as it threw out each completed bunch of oats, and he heard his father's voice as he cracked his long whip.

"Come along there, Dick!" Father called to his horses. "Get up there, Frank! Hurry along, hurry along!"

By the end of the day, Father could only whisper because he had used his voice so much.

Joe and Sam, Henry's brothers, and Steve, the hired man, were busy gathering bundles to set up one shock after another. Then if it rained, the bundles of oats could dry out.

On the last day of harvest, everyone was worried. The sky looked like rain. There might even be a storm. All morning the clouds thickened and the air became heavy.

In the afternoon Uncle Joe finished cutting his own oats and brought his binder over to the farm where Henry lived. Now two binders could work in their large field.

Finally the last bundle of oats was flung from the binder, and Father called "Whoa." He wiped his sweaty face with his big red bandanna handkerchief and looked up at the sky. He had not dared to raise his eyes before.

"Looks a lot like rain," he said.

"Let her rain," Uncle Joe chuckled. "Our worries are over for this year."

That evening at prayer time, Father thanked God for keeping the rain away while the oats were cut and shocked. In his heart Henry also said a thank-you prayer.

# 7

# Threshing Day

Threshing day two weeks later was exciting for Henry. The night before was almost like Christmas Eve; he could hardly wait for morning.

Many neighbors helped. The steam engine would puff away all day. With a long belt, it ran the big threshing machine, which separated the kernels of oats from the bundles of straw. And there would be huge, delicious meals for the whole threshing gang.

Morning came at last. The puffing engine in the cow lot woke his brother Sam. "It's here!" he shouted. "The steam engine is here!"

Henry jumped out of bed at the same

time as Sam. Both of them skipped down the stairs three steps at a time.

They gulped breakfast and hurried out-doors. It was not long until Franz, the engineer, let out a blast from the steam whistle and gave his throttle a slight pull. The engine cylinder began to hiss.

The big belt flip-flapped. The separator cylinder began to hum. When it came to full speed, the hauler tossed on the first bundle of oats, and the big day's work had started.

The engineer was Henry's hero. Like all his brothers and friends, someday Henry wanted to run that steam engine. He daydreamed that he would stand on a high platform back of the throttle just like Franz.

When the outfit moved from one farm to the next, he would draw the long train behind the steam engine. The cylinder cocks would be hissing out floods of steam. Trailing behind would be the water tank, the separator, and the automatic stacker.

He wanted to pass by with all the big and the little folk looking on and waving at him. And he would blast back at them with the steam whistle.

But now Henry's job was taking water

out to the men in the field. They were loading the bundles of oats onto wagons, which brought their loads to the threshing machine.

Henry hitched Flora to an old buggy and took the jug of water and a friend along. Then he drove back and forth between the machine and the men in the field. He could see everything and be everywhere.

Henry stopped to look at the engine. Then he stopped to watch the hustle around the separator at a safe distance from the dust and dirt. At the barn he visited the men scooping kernels of oats from the loaded wagons into the granary.

The men were very glad for a cool drink!

"Thank you, Henry," they said with big smiles as they mopped their faces with their large red bandanna handkerchiefs just like Father's.

Henry's treat was to go to the kitchen where Mother or his cousin Susie gave him a fresh doughnut.

It was play, not work, to go everywhere with Flora.

# 8

# After Threshing

When Henry came back from his last trip, he put Flora in the stable for the night. The sinking red sun made long shadows across the cow lot. The air was getting damp, and the oats were harder to thresh.

The men and the threshing machine worked slower now. The engine puffed angrily sometimes. The heavy black coal smoke rose straight up and floated away like a cloud.

Soon the evening star came into view, and the last forkful of loose straw was pitched onto the platform from the ground.

Father threw his fork over his shoulder. Sam Baily waved his arms. Franz, the engineer, pushed in his throttle and let the whistle shriek with leftover steam. One of the men shoved off the big belt with his fork handle, and the threshing machine stopped working.

With slow steps the men walked toward the house. After they splashed cold water on their faces from the basins in the front yard, they sat down at the table. The men did not talk much while they ate supper because they were so tired.

Afterward, the neighbors hitched up their teams and started for home. They still had their chores to do.

The next day Henry felt lonesome. Everywhere he went, it was so quiet. Father and Joe and Sam had gone to help the neighbors thresh. There was just bread and cold meat to eat instead of mashed potatoes and pie and cake.

"Do you feel lonesome?" Henry asked Johnie as they climbed the two big shining yellow strawstacks.

"*Ja*," said Johnie, "but this is fun."

Henry and Johnie knew the straw was worth a lot. It was feed for the cows and warm beds for them in winter.

Threshing was over. Next year the machine would be back again, and once more Henry would enjoy all the exciting music of machines and men on threshing day.

*144*

# 9

# Henry's Church

Henry and his family belonged to an Amish Mennonite church seven miles from home. One Sunday morning a visiting preacher from Indiana stepped behind the pulpit.

The preacher's name was John S. Coffman. He preached an English sermon. Henry enjoyed hearing him. Usually the services in Henry's church were in the German language.

On the way home for dinner at Henry's house, Brother Coffman told him about the stars. This was one of Henry's favorite studies. Henry also discovered that Brother Coffman liked stories and history just as he did.

As Henry grew up, he learned that Jacob Ammann started the Amish church long ago, in the seventeenth century. This church received part of its name from Jacob Ammann's last name.

Many years ago the Amish were treated cruelly because of their beliefs. The Amish first lived in Europe, and the governments there wanted to decide what people believe and how they worship. Because the Amish did not agree, they suffered many hardships.

Some of the Amish came to America to settle in little communities on the prairies. Among these settlers were Henry's Grandfather Smith and one of his great-grandfathers.

Here in America the government was kind to the Amish. These people were thankful for their freedom to worship God the way they felt was right.

The Amish worshiped in homes. Late in the 1800s, some of the Amish changed and took the name Amish Mennonites. They built their church meetinghouses just as simple as their houses were.

When Henry was twelve, his father became a minister. Later he was bishop of all the Amish Mennonite churches in Illinois.

At night after he had worked hard all day in the fields and most of the family was in bed, Henry's father studied to prepare his sermon. He read from his Bible and from a concordance, which is something like a dictionary.

Sometimes he nodded in his chair and was half asleep, but he would rouse himself and keep working on his Sunday sermon.

"Shouldn't you come to bed?" asked Mother.

"Not yet," said Father as he wiped the sleep from his eyes. "I have a lot of studying to do yet for Sunday."

Father taught Henry and his brothers and sisters that church services were not the only time for thinking about God and his way.

"If you yourselves are good neighbors," he told them, "you will never have any trouble with others on Sunday, or on any other day of the week, either."

Henry was glad for the things Father and his church taught him.

During Henry's boyhood, Sunday school was a new idea in the churches. When he knew his lesson well, his Uncle Chris gave him little colored tickets with Bible verses printed on them. Henry saved them at home and learned the verses by heart.

Uncle Chris also taught him to read German. When Uncle Chris would lean over his shoulder to help him, Henry could feel his beard tickling the back of his neck.

Church services were long, but Henry loved to hear the four-part singing and the tunes of the hymns. As they sat around the dining room table after supper, Father helped his family to sing some of those same songs.

Henry made music himself. At first he had a whistle to blow on. Later he had a mouth organ. He thought this kind of music was the most beautiful of all. He was glad when he could go to singing school on Saturday evenings with the other young people.

# 10

# The Telescope

While Henry went to high school in Metamora, he took astronomy and studied the stars. Oh, how Henry wished for a telescope!

Henry was to be sixteen soon, and Father gave each of his boys a watch for his sixteenth birthday. Henry did not feel that he needed a watch, so he suggested that perhaps Father and Mother could give him a telescope instead.

On his birthday there was a box from Montgomery Ward. In it was a telescope for Henry.

Later in the evening, Henry tried out his telescope. "Look, Father!" he called excitedly. "See the four moons of Jupiter?"

Father looked, and sure enough, there they were. Through the telescope, the moon looked huge. They saw mountains and great plains on the moon.

Every few days Henry noticed spots pass across the sun. He knew it was not safe for him to look at the sun for more than a second or two, or he would harm his eyes.

Through the telescope he could spot stars too faint and far away to see with his eyes alone.

Earth seemed small to Henry now, and he felt small, too. God's creation was exciting, big, and beautiful. What a great God to plan such an interesting world!

Henry's father also liked to use the telescope. He made a tripod to hold it steady and let it be moved in any direction. Henry could look at anything he wished for a long time.

Engineer, carpenter, farmer, astronomer, juggler, teacher. What would Henry be some day?

# 11

# Henry, the Teacher

In a few years the time came for Henry to leave home, but now he had a new name, C. Henry Smith. He thought the name, Henry Smith, needed something added to it, so he decided on a *C.*

For three years he taught grade school near his home. Then a letter came in the mail for Henry. He was asked to be one of the first teachers in the Mennonite school at Elkhart, Indiana.

"You may stay in our home," John S. Coffman wrote to him. "It will be a pleasure to have you live with us."

Henry was glad for this good news because he liked John S. Coffman. He remembered the fine sermon he had

Henry tried out his telescope.

preached in his church one Sunday.

Henry did not go to Indiana in 1898 by train or on a horse. He rode his bicycle all the way! It was a long trip, over 200 miles on roads that were not paved. At last he arrived in Elkhart, tired and dusty.

The Coffmans helped Henry to feel at home right away.

Henry liked the countryside around Elkhart, with its woods and lakes and the St. Joseph River. Henry often rode his bicycle along the winding paths. Indiana was a land of poetry for Henry.

As a new teacher, he read a lot of poems, and he enjoyed helping his students understand what poetry had to say.

"To a Waterfowl" was the title of a poem they studied one day. "God helps us know what to do just as he shows a waterfowl where to go," Henry told his students.

"The waterfowl floats far from danger in the rosy evening sky on its trip alone to its summer home.

"It knows the way to go and flies in a straight path in the sky to get there. God helps it to know. This is called instinct.

"God is waiting to guide us, too, if we ask him to show us the way," added Professor Smith.

Henry also was a teacher at other schools.

He taught at Goshen College in Indiana, at Bluffton College in Ohio for thirty-five years, and at Bethel College in Kansas for one year. He made his dream come true to become a good teacher like Willie Whitmore. And he did something more.

# 12

# Henry, the Author

Later Henry decided to study history at a school in Chicago. He learned that long ago Menno Simons was one of the leaders of the Mennonites.

Henry believed that war was wrong and tried to practice Jesus Christ's way of peace. How pleased he was to find that his forefathers and foremothers had gone ahead of him on the same path of faith he was following!

Sometimes he had thought the Amish Mennonites had odd ideas. He had felt ashamed that they were so different from other people. Now he knew God had led them after all, in the way of love and peace and simple living.

Henry decided that the beliefs and way of life of the Mennonites were important for everyone to know about. He wanted to share the story about the Mennonites with anyone ready to listen or read.

And that is just what he did! He wrote an interesting book called *The Story of the Mennonites*. When you are older, you can read this book yourself.

In another book, *Mennonite Country Boy*, Henry told about his own early life. He wrote parts of many books and magazines. His chief interest was in the Mennonites, and he was an important writer of Mennonite history.

Through his books and pieces in magazines, Henry was able to reach many more people than he could teach in his classrooms. So he went even farther than his dream as a boy to be a teacher in a schoolhouse. He also became a writer—Henry, the author, teacher of the world.

• • •

Your parents and teachers may read about C. Henry Smith in *The Mennonite Encyclopedia,* volume 4 (Herald Press, 1959), Smith's *Mennonite Country Boy* (Newton, Kansas: Faith and Life Press, 1962), or *The Story of the Mennonites* (Berne, 1941).

# The Author

*The author with her husband, Milton, who often edits the stories and articles she writes.*

Geraldine Gross Harder grew up in Doylestown, Pennsylvania, near the homes of Christopher Dock and David Rittenhouse, about whom she writes in this book. She and her husband, Milton, have more than once visited the Mennonite farming community of Weierhof, Germany, from which Christian Krehbiel came. Also, the Amish country of C. Henry Smith and the colleges in which he later taught are familiar territory to Geraldine.

While single Geraldine was an elementary teacher, writer, and editor of primary Sunday school curriculum. After her marriage to Milton Harder, who is a pastor, she has been a homemaker and has continued to write. Presently the Harders live in North Newton, Kansas, and are members of the Alexanderwohl Mennonite Church, Goessel, Kansas. They have two married sons. Bob teaches at Hesston College and Jim teaches at Bethel College.

The Harders spent five years in Europe, serving under the Mennonite Central Committee. Among other places, they lived in Seattle, Washington, for thirteen years. They enjoy traveling and learning to know people and how they live.

Geraldine, especially, enjoys history and asks Milton to stop at every historical marker; with a note pad in hand, she jots down information she wants to remember for a possible story or article. Geraldine likes to make history live. She feels that the more we know about our past, the more meaningful our present and future life will be.

Many church papers have published Geraldine's stories and essays. She wrote *When Apples Are Ripe* (Herald Press,

1971), the story of Clayton Kratz, a Mennonite Central Committee volunteer who disappeared in Russia in 1920 while helping suffering people. With her husband she is coauthor of *Christmas Goose* (Faith and Life Press, 1990), about a young Hutterite girl who had a pet goose.

Geraldine says that Christopher Dock, David Rittenhouse, C. Henry Smith, and Christian Krehbiel have much to share that can be helpful to us today. For example, we can pray for each other like Christopher prayed for his pupils.

Geraldine likes to quote the verse by Henry Wadsworth Longfellow:

Lives of great men all remind us
  We can make our lives sublime,
And, departing, leave behind us
  Footprints on the sands of time.

# The Illustrator

Holly Hannon lives in Greenville, South Carolina, where she grew up. She loves animals, cooking, and pioneer books such as *Little House on the Prairie.*

In the fourth grade Holly already knew that she wanted to be an artist. After high school she graduated from Ringling School of Art and Design in Sarasota, Florida. She has prepared many illustrations for children's stories and other books.

Holly likes to help prepare books that honor God. She is a member of Southside Baptist Church, Greenville.